Acting Edition

Merry Me

by Hansol Jung

FOR PRODUCTION INQUIRIES

UNITED STATES AND CANADA
info@concordtheatricals.com
1-866-979-0447

UNITED KINGDOM AND EUROPE
licensing@concordtheatricals.co.uk
020-7054-7298

Each title is subject to availability from Concord Theatricals Corp., depending upon country of performance. Please be aware that *MERRY ME* may not be licensed by Concord Theatricals Corp. in your territory. Professional and amateur producers should contact the nearest Concord Theatricals Corp. office or licensing partner to verify availability.

No one shall make any changes in this title(s) for the purpose of production. No part of this book may be reproduced, stored in a retrieval system, scanned, uploaded, or transmitted in any form, by any means, now known or yet to be invented, including mechanical, electronic, digital, photocopying, recording, videotaping, or otherwise, without the prior written permission of the publisher. No one shall share this title(s), or any part of this title(s), through any social media or file hosting websites.

For all inquiries regarding first class stage performance,motion picture, television, online/digital and other media rights, please contact Kevin Lin at Creative Artists Agency.

MUSIC AND THIRD-PARTY MATERIALS USE NOTE

Licensees are solely responsible for obtaining formal written permission from copyright owners to use copyrighted music and/or other copyrighted third-party materials (e.g. artworks, logos) in the performance of this play and are strongly cautioned to do so. If no such permission is obtained by the licensee, then the licensee must use only original music and materials that the licensee owns and controls. Licensees are solely responsible and liable for clearances of all third-party copyrighted materials, including without limitation music, and shall indemnify the copyright owners of the play(s) and their licensing agent, Concord Theatricals Corp., against any costs, expenses, losses and liabilities arising from the use of such copyrighted third-party materials by licensees. For music, please contact the appropriate music licensing authority in your territory for the rights to any incidental music.

IMPORTANT BILLING AND CREDIT REQUIREMENTS

If you have obtained performance rights to this title, please refer to your licensing agreement for important billing and credit requirements.

MERRY ME had its world premiere at New York Theatre Workshop (Patricia McGregor, Artistic Director) in New York City on October 11th, 2023. The performance was directed by Leigh Silverman, with sets by Rachel Hauck, costume design by Alejo Vietti, lighting design by Barbara Samuels, and sound design by Kate Marvin and Caroline Eng. The cast was as follows:

LT. SHANE HORNE . . . . Esco Jouléy

DR. JESS O'NOPE . . . . .Marinda Anderson

MRS. SAPPH MEMNON . . . . Nicole Villamil

PVT. WILLY MEMNON . . . . .Ryan Spahn

GENERAL MEMNON . . . . David Ryan Smith

GENERAL'S WIFE . . . . .Cindy Cheung

THE ANGEL . . . . .Shaunette Renée Wilson

CHARACTERS

LT. SHANE HORNE – God's gift to lady parts of all shapes, colors and vintages.

DR. JESS O'NOPE – An unwilling Prophet.

MRS. SAPPH MEMNON – An unwilling wife.

PVT. WILLY MEMNON – A very woke male partner to Sapph.

GENERAL MEMNON – A war-starved General.

GENERAL'S WIFE – A sex-starved wife.

THE ANGEL – From Tony Kushner's *Angels in America*.

SOME OTHERS – Doubled by principal cast.

SETTING

Naval Basecamp of a Nation's Most Prestigious Navy on an Island Not Far from Another Nation's Most Vulnerable Coast Cities.

TIME

The year of an Ongoing War.

For Leigh

Pre-Show

(A Very Gay Playlist bops the audience into the lobby and house.[1])

(When the time is right:)

ANGEL. Welcome to our play *Merry Me*. Written by Hansol; directed by Leigh.[2] David[3] is Aga Memnon, Cindy[4] is Mrs. Memnon, Nicole[5] plays Mrs. Sappho Memnon with Ryan[6] as Private Willy Memnon, her very woke male partner. Those are our Memnons. Marinda[7] is our prophet; and Esco[8] is God's gift to lady parts of all shapes, colors and vintages, as usual. And I play me, the Angel. You're welcome. The name of the town is Classified for government purposes, latitude redacted degrees redacted minutes; longitude redacted degrees redacted minutes, at the Naval Basecamp of a Nation's Most Prestigious Navy on an Island Not Far from Another Nation's Most Vulnerable Coast Cities. The Day is a crisp spring day in the Year of an Ongoing War. The time is just before dawn.

*(A rooster crows. It's the **ANGEL**. She crows.)*

---

1. A license to produce *Merry Me* does not include a performance license for any third-party or copyrighted music. Licensees should create an original composition or use music in the public domain. For further information, please see the Music and Third-Party Materials Use Note on page iii.
2. Name of director
3. Name of performer playing **GENERAL**
4. Name of performer playing **WIFE**
5. Name of performer playing **SAPPHO**
6. Name of performer playing **WILLY**
7. Name of performer playing **O'NOPE**
8. Name of performer playing **HORNE**

ANGEL. The sky is beginning to show some streaks of light over in the East there, where the sea meets the sky. The Morning Star always gets wonderful bright the minute before it has to go, doesn't it?

> (**ANGEL** *stares at it for a moment.*)

It takes a great deal of focus to imagine a disappearing bright Morning Star while staring at a blinding spotlight but that, is the job of the actor. Which you have come to see today. So here it is again:

> (**ANGEL** *stares at the Morning Star again.*
> *A moment of great acting.*)

Pretty good, huh?

Well, I better show you how our camp lies. Miles and miles of sandy beach lies dotted by Naval tents filled with men and women of the great nation, waiting for the order to launch their little lives into a fight to the death.

It takes a great deal of focus to imagine miles and miles of sandy beach dotted by Naval tents while trapped inside a dark room with a small patch of stage space that indicates as much but that, is the job of the audience. Which you have come to do today. So give it a go.

> (**ANGEL** *gestures the beach to life for the* *audience.*)

> (*They do their job of imagination.*)

Very good. Now with that in mind, please take a moment to turn off your phones, mind the exits, and the other things good theatergoers know to do once the houselights go down. Because, here they go. Down.

The Great Plan

ANGEL. And now we're in the Doctor's office.

O'NOPE. You can't be serious.

HORNE. I am.

O'NOPE. People will be upset.

HORNE. I know.

O'NOPE. It will ruin your reputation.

HORNE. That's the point.

O'NOPE. You will destroy your legacy. And likely, mine as well –

HORNE. My mind is made up Doctor Jess O'Nope. I came to you with the proposal, my most able surgeon, most treasured friend, my first and best fuck,

O'NOPE. I am not –

HORNE. Fine, not first but okay fuck, but to be fair you still thought you were straight -

O'NOPE. No, I was saying I am not a surgeon. I am a psychiatrist.

HORNE. Really?

O'NOPE. What do you think you and I have been doing all these months in my office?

HORNE. I thought you do both.

O'NOPE. Both? You really want your shrink to do your open heart surgeries?

HORNE. It's war. Everyone is multitasking.

O'NOPE. If you are questioning the value I bring to –

HORNE. I am not questioning, I am asking a question and the question I am asking, you already have been asked.

This is a rare moment of need from me to you. Doctor Jess O'Nope, or rather, Just Jess O'Nope,

O'NOPE. I'm still a doctor.

HORNE. Jess. Is it a Jes? Or is it a No.

O'NOPE. It is a No. I'm not going to get caught up in another of your bonkers schemes based off a baseless theory –

HORNE. Maybe bonkers but Not baseless! While I was in solitary confinement, I read up on this –

O'NOPE. How did you get reading material in solitary confinement?

HORNE. Slept with Ethel.

O'NOPE. The guard?

HORNE. She feels unseen and underappreciated and appreciated my interest in her.

And my finger, in her also.

O'NOPE. Weren't you put in for having sexed up the general's wife?

HORNE. Yes I was.

O'NOPE. Why are you like this?

HORNE. It is a gift and a curse. Are you too in need of the Merries, Doctor? You look like you are in need. You know I am always at the ready to provide for those in need.

O'NOPE. Don't even start that shit with me.

HORNE. I am impressed, Doctor Jess O'Nope. For I sense it has been a while for you.

O'NOPE. Shane, I am tired, I've had a long day, and as much as I would love to help you, what you are proposing, is just Not how one reaches an orgasm.

HORNE. Yes it is! It is for me! In the reading material that Emily got me.

O'NOPE. Ethel.

HORNE. Ethel's the night guard, Emily's the day shift. Ethel told Emily about, and then Emily wanted, and after I gave them what they wanted –

O'NOPE. Together?

HORNE. Separately and then together.

O'NOPE. Of course.

HORNE. After twice together and once more separately, they together got me what I wanted.

O'NOPE. I love that for you.

HORNE. Doc. I've long confessed to you my failure to give myself the Merries.

O'NOPE. Can we not call it that?

HORNE. All my life, I've been fretting and sweating to fulfill my God-given mission, the mission to provide Merries to ladyparts of all shapes, colors, and vintages – and in that endeavor have allowed my own ladyparts to succumb to the numbness.

O'NOPE. So you were what, rubbing up on prison books hoping to come?

HORNE. Of course not! I mean, yes *The Complete Works of Shakespeare* is great for those discovery years between the ages of seven and eleven: my *William* was rubbed practically spineless,

O'NOPE. Oh for me it was *The Complete Illustrated Bible for Adults*.

HORNE. Bible?

O'NOPE. That is what was available to me.

O'NOPE. Please continue your story of raping government literature for your orgasm.

HORNE. Not raping, Reading. In a desperate search I was perusing the ancient texts of *Kama Sutra*, Archives from Priestesses of the Assyrian Temple, research material from the writers' room of *L Word* –

O'NOPE. *Generation Q?*

HORNE. What? Ew! No the original.

O'NOPE. You haters are why all our shows are getting cancelled. I thought it was fine.

HORNE. It was not fine. Also not fine was my research, which is the point of this scene, will you please stay focused.

O'NOPE. Sorry.

HORNE. Nothing worked. I was exhausted, frustrated, coming up dry for days until, enter, Mister Harry Horner.

O'NOPE. That was your inspo? He sounds like a straight white male person.

HORNE. A straight white male restoration comedy person. Harry Horner gets his straight white male restoration comedy penis all up in all the women in town. Their husbands find out, locks it down and so Harry is having trouble getting any. Enter his genius friend The Doctor.

(*Despite herself,* **O'NOPE** *kinda likes this.*)

O'NOPE. There's a doctor in the story.

HORNE. Genius Doctor. He tells everyone that Harry's dick is broken! The guys are disarmed, the girls are concerned, Harry gets so much sex, because when the ladies come to see if it is really broken, surprise! It is not! Sexytime.

And this sex is better than any other sex because it took five acts to get there.

O'NOPE. I don't understand how this relates to you getting an orgasm.

HORNE. What do you mean you don't understand, it's so clear. I need my five acts of my fake broken penis to get to my merry. I need my Act One we have sad broken pussy, I cannot do the sex, Act Two, cannot do the sex even more, Act Three, so much no sex it hurts, more of that in Act Four to Act Five what had been lost has been recovered by a caring, inquisitive vagina-lover. Merries for Me! End of Play.

O'NOPE. Why can't your pussy break to something less complicated? Yeast infection? Gonorrhea? Just a mysterious, bicycle-ish, accident?

HORNE. I need a problem of the mind, not the machine. This is how it must be. You must tell all the World! Lieutenant Shane Horne has been zapped, nuked and lobotomized and returned to the world as Straight as a Road through Nevada!

(Thunder and lightning!)

(**O'NOPE** *waits for it to pass.)*

(It does.)

O'NOPE. Shane, gay conversion therapy is not a real thing. It's a dangerous, dishonest, and violent practice discredited by modern medicine,

HORNE. You don't actually have to do it. You're just Saying that you've done it.

O'NOPE. I could lose my medical license.

HORNE. We do not live in a world where people lose licenses for traumatizing a gay person's psyche and even if you do lose your job, you hate it. You'd love to finally quit and find out what you really wanted to do with your life before you caved to your father's wishes and went to medical school for his approval that you never got.

O'NOPE. I love my job.

HORNE. Jess. Don't be the female past her prime who has
    been single for a decade,

O'NOPE. I have not been single for a –

HORNE. making out with a drunk bachelor at his bachelor
    party at two a.m. does not count as a date.

O'NOPE. Yes it does because I have since developed a,
    actually pretty deep level of affection for –

HORNE. Willy Memnon?

O'NOPE. Yes.

HORNE. Wow, you really do love a project.

O'NOPE. People get off on different things.

HORNE. Jess. Don't be this person. Be the person who
    grabs her prime back. Grab it by the pussy! Take the
    risk! Join me on this quest! Be the Prophet to pave the
    way for my Merries! Okay fine say yes and I'll go to hot
    yoga with you.

O'NOPE. No way.

HORNE. Yes way. Yes. Way. That will be the price of my
    Merries and it will be worth every sweaty, pointlessly
    suffocating, terribly humiliating minute of those...two
    sessions.

O'NOPE. Five.

HORNE. Fine. Four.

O'NOPE. Fine. Ten.

HORNE. Okay Okay Okay Jesus. Ten. You'll do it for Ten?

O'NOPE. I'll do it for ten.

HORNE. She'll do it for ten!!!!!!

> (**HORNE** *does the "she will do it for ten hot
> yoga sessions" dance.*)

Jessica. Thank you.

> (**HORNE** *kisses her, a deep, in-the-throat, hot, beautiful, a could-this-feeling-please-go-on-forever-but-also-I-feel-I-need-to-pee-most-immediately kind of kiss...)*

> (**HORNE** *pulls away and beams with gratitude.)*

> (**O'NOPE** *quietly holds herself from wanting more.)*

O'NOPE. You're welcome.

> (**HORNE** *leaves.)*

> (**O'NOPE** *takes a deep breath of a levitated woman coming back to earth –)*

> (*She pulls out a cheerfully-colored vibrating rabbit.)*

> (*With a slight nod to the audience, leaves the stage to be with her rabbit.)*

ANGEL. Want to tell you something about our girl Jessica there. Awful bright, top of her class, captain of the Dungeons and Dragons league. Loves to say she tops from the bottom but her bottom's been untopped for some time now. Little does she know, her prime is yet to come. We've got –

*(To **CREW MEMBER** who has begun to change the set.)* Hey (Crew Member).

(To audience.) Please join me in the corner of the stage so they can set up the next scene while I distract you with my acting.

Now, as I was saying –

(And we hear female sex sounds.)

ANGEL. We've got some straight people on base too, hear it?

(And we hear some male sex sounds…)

Familiar to some, to some others less so.

To get us all on the same page, how about I give us a bird's eye view of the situation?

Married People Sex

(We are now with a straight couple having sex.)

(Female sex sounds continue as do the male sex sounds...)

WILLY. O Mrs. Memnon.

SAPPH. You can do it Willy.

WILLY. O Mrs. Memnon.

SAPPH. Willy you are so close.

WILLY. O O O Mrs. Memnon.

SAPPH. Come on Willy I believe in you.

WILLY. O O Mrs. Memnon. I am coming coming I am come...d.

(He comes, collapses.)

*(***SAPPH*** turns on her brightly-colored vibrator.)*

(Bzz bzz bzbzbz Bzz bzz bzbzbz.)

*(***WILLY*** waits.)*

(Bzz bzz bzbzbz Bzz bzz bzb –)

*(With a tidy and polite moan, ***SAPPH*** finishes and they cuddle.)*

O Mrs. Memnon.

SAPPH. That was nice.

WILLY. Thank you Mrs. Memnon. How was it for you, Mrs. Memnon?

SAPPH. Hon?

WILLY. Yes?

SAPPH. I know you're happy we're married and all and it
is really very sweet but it gets a bit weird when you call
me that during sex.

WILLY. Mrs. Memnon?

SAPPH. Yeah it's a little, that's what people call your mom.

WILLY. That's not what I call my mom?

SAPPH. Yeah I know, maybe how about let's not during sex.

WILLY. Okay.

SAPPH. Cool.

WILLY. No problemo.

SAPPH. Thank you.

(*They cuddle.*)

WILLY. I'm not calling my mom during sex tho? I'm calling
you. I'm secure enough in my masculinity to be able to
call to Mrs. Memnon and not think of my mother while
I make love to my wife, you know?

SAPPH. Totally. I know. It's just weird for me.

WILLY. I know. I'm just saying.

SAPPH. Thank you for saying.

WILLY. You are very welcome.

(*They cuddle.*)

You know while we are on the subject of what we call
each other during sex?

SAPPH. Uh huh?

WILLY. I'm wondering about, you know,

SAPPH. You don't like it when I call you Willy?

WILLY. Mmmnot my favorite?

SAPPH. But it's so cute.

WILLY. Mmmmaybe a bit too cute?

SAPPH. But it's so you.

WILLY. Yeah? Yeah okay.

SAPPH. I could totally not if you'd rather not.

WILLY. Yeah, no, you know, I'd rather you not.

SAPPH. Okay.

WILLY. Awesome. Thank you.

SAPPH. No problemo.

WILLY. Great. Hey! Look at us getting through early marital conflicts like a boss.

(They high-five.)

(A sweet married-people kiss.)

I want to be a good man for you Sapphy.

SAPPH. You are, Willy, am.

WILLY. I want to give you pleasure Sapphy.

SAPPH. I know you do.

WILLY. I'm trying.

SAPPH. I know you are.

WILLY. Okay, but any time you have thoughts, know that I'm always open to dialogue /

SAPPH. Really? Coz I was thinking about – you know the Red Room in *Fifty Shades*, right?

WILLY. Oh gross. Are you really into, did you really read –?

Sorry. Hey. As long as it's like, you know, like, safe. We can talk about it. Any Time.

SAPPH. Like right now?

WILLY. I mean, not right now? I'm not super in the mood to discuss your need to give me pain to get off.

SAPPH. Oh. Okay.

WILLY. Sorry. I'm just saying I would love to make you want me as much as I want you.

SAPPH. You *do* want me an awful lot now that we have landed here on the Naval Base Not so Far from the Vulnerable Coasts of the Enemy Nation.

WILLY. Our forces have been stationed here for months since the Electric Blackout. Our fleets can't start their engines, no one can call their mothers, or watch porn.

SAPPH. It's odd how vibrators are the only electric devices that still work. Not complaining, but odd.

WILLY. Whether vibrators work or not are the least of our worries Sapphy.

SAPPHY. For you yes, for me no.

WILLY. The General can't get his war. The soldiers are restless and full of pent-up feelings of violence. And in the middle of all this mess here you are, so pure, so beautiful, so willing to not call me Willy during sex. I can't believe my luck that you are here with me.

SAPPH. Yes you are so lucky to be the General's son.

WILLY. Come on, Sapphy, it's not like that. I know I'm just a Private, but I have great potential is why I have been allowed a special glamping tent and permission to bring my bride to war! Why else do you think I have been called to this Island to fix the Blackout?

SAPPH. You really still believe you have been called to this Island to fix the Blackout?

WILLY. Sapphy. The Angel whispered in my ear, "You are the one Willy. You will fix the Blackout. You will pack your bags, go to the Naval Base Not so Far From the Vulnerable Coasts of the Enemy Nation and save your father, and the world with him." She said that, Word. For. Word.

SAPPH. Yes and then we woke up in a puddle of your ejaculations.

WILLY. *(Remembering fondly.)* Yes we did.

SAPPH. So, any ideas on how you'll do it?

WILLY. It'll come to me. When the time is right.

SAPPH. Such confidence my love.

WILLY. My mother always said a man without confidence might as well be one without a pecker.

SAPPH. What a great motherly thing to say.

ANGEL. Ah Mothers. Fountain of Life. Foundation of society. Owners of ladyparts that have seen the ninth circle of hell and yet still search for paradise. Here is one such lady and her parts, right now.

GENERAL. O Mrs. Memnon.

WIFE. Don't call me that.

GENERAL. O Mrs. Memnon.

WIFE. Cut it out I said.

GENERAL. O O O Mrs.

(*Slap.*)

Ow. Why?

WIFE. That's what people call your mother. It's gross.

GENERAL. Is it so wrong for a grown man to need his mother's love and care from time to time?

WIFE. You really want me answer that?

(A moment.)

(Then he starts to climb back on her.)

GENERAL. O Mrs. –

*(**WIFE** pushes him aside.)*

Why? Why?!

WIFE. Not really in the mood any more.

GENERAL. But it is your duty! How am I to have my war if my pecker does not work? It is your job to make it work woman! Your god-given occupation as a –

WIFE. I resign.

(She pulls out a vibrator.)

(Bzz bzz bzbzbz, bzz bzz bzbzbz...)

*(The **GENERAL** watches helplessly, and then starts to pull on his little guy.)*

(Squeak squeak squeak.)

(It's a competitive medley of who will get to their Merries before the other:)

(Bzz bzz bzbzbz, bzz bzz bzbzbz...)

(Squeak squeak squeak...)

*(**WIFE** wins.)*

(A tidy and polite moan, and the vibrating stops.)

(Squeak squeak.)

(Squeak.)

*(**GENERAL** gives up and stares accusingly at his penis...)*

GENERAL. You disappoint me.

(An authoritative knock. Which is weird because where is the door to this glamping tent?)

Yes?

O'NOPE. Sir, this is Doctor O'Nope. I just had some reporting to report.

*(**GENERAL** looks at his watch.)*

GENERAL. Right now?

O'NOPE. General Memnon, it's about Lieutenant Horne.

*(**WIFE**'s attention piques, eager and curious.)*

GENERAL. The bitch is out, huh?

O'NOPE. Yes sir. But upon exit interview I found we have accomplished the most unbelievable thing.

(Back at Private Willy's special glamping tent.)

(A cute little bell rattles.)

(It is connected to a paper cup telephone.)

GENERAL. *(On the paper cup telephone.)* Private Memnon. Come in. Over.

WILLY. It's the General! I wonder what he wants.

(On paper cup telephone.) This is Private Memnon sir. Listening sir. Over.

(Cute little bell.)

GENERAL. *(On paper cup.)* Come over. Over.

WILLY. *(On paper cup.)* To where? Excuse me? To where sir? Hello?

(Cute little bell.)

GENERAL. *(On paper cup.)* You have to say over. Over.

WILLY. *(On paper cup.)* Over.

(Cute little bell.)

GENERAL. *(On paper cup.)* Come to my barracks. I have a special mission for you. Over.

WILLY. *(On paper cup.)* A mission!? Yes sir! I'll be right over! Over and out.

(He starts putting his clothes on.)

SAPPH. A special Mission! How exciting!

WILLY. I'm pumped. I'll finally get to show Dad that I'm worthy of the Memnon name.

SAPPH. Hooray! It's all you've ever wanted all the years of your privileged yet unremarkable life! Can I come along to bear witness?

WILLY. You know, I think it would be wise of us to pick the right time to introduce you to everybody.

SAPPH. Pretty please?

WILLY. I don't know, Sapphy. People have been sitting around with hormones filling up their system, and it's just not the best time to show a new female face.

SAPPH. Come on, it can't be that bad? There are so many women on the camp. I've seen them!

WILLY. Honestly, I am more worried about the women then I am about the men. They are not your average G.I. Janes looking for their appropriate Joes if you know what I mean.

SAPPH. William! I didn't take you for a homophobe.

WILLY. I'm not! Oh god no! I love the gays. I am an ally of the gays, through and through I swear. Like, I had my share of gay moments in high school and everything!

SAPPH. Ho. Say more.

(He decides to not.)

WILLY. What I mean about the women, here, that, they aren't like the average –,

I was speaking really specifically about this one Lieutenant,

Okay so, Before we were even married, when I was out here by myself, you know?

SAPPH. I do know.

WILLY. I made the mistake of showing her a picture of you, and then she started following your account, remembered your birthday, star sign, the color of your eyes –

SAPPH. *(Surprisingly pleased.)* She did?

WILLY. She wouldn't stop going on and on about how she liked the way your selfies are all the same angle but you make it special and different every time –

SAPPH. *(More pleased.)* She did not.

WILLY. Honestly I found it a little intrusive and a lot creepy.

SAPPH. Yeah. Totally. That's really weird. She sounds really weird. Is she hot?

WILLY. Oh god no, unless you're like, into strong female leaders with a piercing gaze and massive biceps.

SAPPH. Hm.

(Cute little bell.)

GENERAL. *(On paper cup.)* What the fuck is taking so long, over!

WILLY. I should go.

SAPPH. You know what, Mr. Memnon?

WILLY. Uh oh.

SAPPH. I have an idea.

WILLY. No, Sapph.

SAPPH. You know that no is the opposite thing to say to me when you don't want me to do something.

WILLY. But if I say yes you'll do it.

SAPPH. Yes I will.

WILLY. So I can't win.

SAPPH. No. But lucky for you I have a really good idea that will satiate my need to get some air, and your need to keep me hidden from the hormonal paws of your colleagues.

WILLY. Listening.

SAPPH. Dress me in your clothes, and tell people I am your brother-in-law.

WILLY. That is the most opposite of a good idea!

SAPPH. I'll be in boy drag, and Nobody – not male nor female – will have even the remotest interest in me.

WILLY. Have you never ever met a lesbian?

> (**SAPPH** *is putting on Willy's civilian clothes as he protests.*)

SAPPH. I'll need a belt, or suspenders or – actually, it almost all fits!

WILLY. No. Stop it. Sapphy!

SAPPH. Isn't it funny how we are almost the same size?

WILLY. Hilarious. Sapphy. Take my pants off.

SAPPH. Later, Hon. If you behave. ;)

WILLY. Sapph. Come on. I'm serious. I have to –

SAPPH. Tada!

> (**SAPPH** *is all dressed up in Willy's clothes
> and could almost pass for a boy.*)

WILLY. Oh my god why do you look so Cute! Come here.

> (*A kiss of a less-married kind.*)

SAPPH. You like this?

WILLY. Me like this.

SAPPH. If you let me take this out, maybe later I'll let you
take this off...?

WILLY. With my mouth?

SAPPH. With your mouth.

WILLY. From the back?

SAPPH. From the back.

WILLY. And then can we do butt stuff.

SAPPH. You drive a hard bargain Private.

WILLY. It's very hard to be a Private.

SAPPH. I wouldn't know, but I'm sure you'll teach me.

> (*A kiss of a less-married kind.*)

WILLY. If you insist –

> (*Cute little bell.*)

GENERAL. (*On paper cup.*) Stop fucking your wife and
come over asshole. Over.

SAPPH. That's nice.

> (*They straighten up.*)

(Knock knock.)

(And they are outside the General's lodgings.)

WILLY. General? General Memnon?

(Knock knock.)

SAPPH. Doesn't he prefer you to enter through the back door?

WILLY. You're right, he does. My wife is so smart.

*(They start going around to the window, and there, partially hidden by shrubs, is **HORNE**, trying to eavesdrop into the conversation in the house.)*

No!

SAPPH. What?

WILLY. Oh no! I forgot my, pen.

SAPPH. I have a pen.

WILLY. I need my special pen. I need my special pen which helps me feel very special and I need to feel special right now with my special pen which is back in our tent so we should turn back to go –

HORNE. Private William Memnon!

WILLY. Lieutenant Horne! So Good to see you are back from solitary confinement after having been found having sex with my mother!

HORNE. Thank you thank you! Good to see you too. I know it might seem peculiar that I am stationed beneath the General's window like I am eavesdropping on a classified conversation going on with the Doctor and your father, however, I was not.

WILLY. Great! I'll leave you to it.

(**HORNE** *sees* **SAPPH**.)

(*Special Love Jingle. [It would be nice if it was the* **ANGEL** *making the Love Jingle sound.]*)

HORNE. Hello.

SAPPH. Hi.

HORNE. And how are you today?

SAPPH. I am very fine. You?

HORNE. Fine. Also very fine.

WILLY. Me too, very very very fine! I've never been better. And although I would love to continue to share our state of well-beings with each other, we really must get going.

HORNE. Memnon. I heard you got hitched to that beautiful lady of yours, and that she is here with us, yes?

WILLY. Oh no Lieutenant, unfortunately, no.

HORNE. You did not get married? Am I to believe she is then free to singlely mingle?

WILLY. No! Married, yes. Here, no. I know everyone was very excited to meet her, you, in particular, but sadly she got down with a very nasty case of the, uh, leprosy.

HORNE & SAPPH. The leprosy?

WILLY. The leprosy. Yes. Nose falling off, smelly as sin, everyone is very upset. Please, keep us in your prayers. Thank you. Let's go Sapph – bastian, dear brother-in-law.

HORNE. She has a brother!

SAPPH. She does. It's me. Hello.

HORNE. I am so sorry to hear about the leprosy. My deepest condolences.

SAPPH. Thank you.

HORNE. I will pray that God heals, and that He will keep the disease away from her most luminescent cheeks, her limestone-smooth forehead,

WILLY. Thank you for your prayers.

SAPPH. You speak as if you know her.

HORNE. I am sad to say I have never had the chance to meet her, no. Private Memnon here keeps his loved ones very close, and I do not blame him. For, if his wife is anywhere close to being as beautiful as you, dear youthful Mister Saphastian, I would –

SAPPH. What would you do?

HORNE. I mean, what wouldn't I do to be near her radiance, to bask in her brilliance? My good sir Saphastian I would walk a thousand miles just to be there by her side, breathing the same air as she.

WILLY. Can't. She's contagious. You'd die.

SAPPH. You would.

HORNE. I would. And I would die again and again to see her beauty stay in this world unscathed by anything so vile as leprosy, plastic surgery, or marriage. Please, when you see your sister again, do pass on this message of condolences, from my blistering heart to her iridescent lips.

> (**HORNE** *kisses* **SAPPH**. *Everyone is very turned on, even* **WILLY**, *against his will.)*

> (*Love Jingle intensifies.)*

> (*Back in the General's quarters.)*

GENERAL. This is unbelievable. Doctor. We are certain?

O'NOPE. I think so.

GENERAL. Do we think so ninety percent or do we know so hundred percent.

My entire army is at stake here, Doctor. I am very serious about sending this otherwise superb and shapely-shouldered soldier to be court-martialed for her heretically heterophobic courting habits, by unscientifically citing some clause that can be jiu-jitsued into damning evidence that she should be stripped of her glowing titles, medals, and pension plan, leaving her with no future prospects but a short drug-addled life on the inner city streets. I wouldn't want to include an otherwise decently-daughtered Doctor on the docket for malignant misinformation.

O'NOPE. You know. Um. Hundred percent is a very tricky percentage in the world of science sir...

> (**O'NOPE** *looks out the window, sees* **HORNE** *deeply making out with* **SAPPH**.)

> (*Intensified Love Jingle returns.*)

Oh woah.

> (*The* **GENERAL** *sees this too. His mouth hangs open in incredulous surprise.*)

> (*A moment of tension where this could land either way...*)

GENERAL. Am I seeing what I am seeing?

O'NOPE. Depends... What are you seeing?

GENERAL. I never thought I would live to see it. You've turned Shane Horne into a heterosexual soldier.

> (*Thunder and lighting!*)

> (**WIFE**'s *face falls.*)

GENERAL. Congratulations Doctor. I will recommend you for a raise, a promotion, medals of valor and whatever else you want. *(To* **WILLY***.)* Private Memnon!

WILLY. Dad! I mean, sir General sir! I am here to receive the special mission sir.

GENERAL. I wanted you to secretly spy on Shane to see to it she doesn't fuck with my woman and if it seems she is doing so to put a bullet in her head but clearly it's all been solved so you may go back to playing husband and wife! And tell your mrs. memnon to come say hey. Lieutenant Horne!

HORNE. Yes General!

GENERAL. Welcome to our team. The sex is meh to middling to fine but the basic human rights package rocks. Over and out.

ANGEL. And out goes the General, overjoyed at the fact that he won't have to send his otherwise superb and shapely-shouldered soldier to be court-martialed for her heretically heterophobic courting habits, by unscientifically citing some clause that can be jiu-jitsued into damning evidence that she should be stripped of her glowing titles, medals, and pension plan, leaving her with no future prospects but a short drug-addled life on the inner city streets. All is very well. Or is it?

Because back in the privacy of the Doctor's office…

Horne Begins a Climb

(Back in the Doctor's office.)

HORNE. I can't believe it. He was really serious about sending me, his otherwise superb and shapely-shouldered soldier to be court-martialed for my heretically heterophobic courting habits, by unscientifically citing some clause that can be jiu-jitsued into damning evidence that I should be stripped of my glowing titles, medals, and pension plan, leaving me with no future prospects but a short drug-addled life on the inner city streets?

O'NOPE. Yup.

HORNE. That's cold.

O'NOPE. He is a General with a full fleet and no internet to have his war. And then you fucked his wife. The man is at the tip of his impotent wits, Shane. This is no longer a simple plot to find your Merries. It's no longer about ten, friendship-building, spirit-enhancing, muscle-toning sessions of hot yoga. If he finds out I lied about your sexuality, we're dead.

HORNE. Wow.

O'NOPE. I know. But there's no need to panic just yet. There are certain measures we can take, right now, to get you discharged with honors but we have to do it quickly before –

HORNE. I really. I just, I couldn't have asked for anything so delicious. Really what a good conflict needs is a formidable antagonist that stands in the way of my super objective and really I don't know that even Shonda Rhimes could have done any better!

O'NOPE. Shane! This isn't a joke! Laws and regulations that protect non-heteronormative citizens are still at infant stage and can easily be loopholed or repealed by angry impotent men with nuclear power at their finger–

(**HORNE** *holds a gentle finger to* **O'NOPE**'s *protesting lips.)*

HORNE. Shh. Jessie.

O'NOPE. Shane.

HORNE. Do you hear that?

O'NOPE. The sound of two women living out a small and short humiliating life which is bound to end with their heads in the ovens or stones in their pockets if not via the run-of-the-mill vengeful heteronormative rage? Yes. Yes I do. It's us.

HORNE. It's the sound of my tiny-baby merry seeding, taking soil.

O'NOPE. Shane c'mon!

HORNE. The tickle that which I felt when kissing that hottie in boy drag has blossomed into a – I have to go.

O'NOPE. Where?

HORNE. I have to get my Shakespeare before the tickles leave me.

(*She runs off while* **O'NOPE** *calls after her.*)

O'NOPE. Stay away from the General's wife, okay? Okay?!

(*But* **HORNE** *is gone.*)

It's okay.

We're just gonna,

What are we just gonna

We are

Breathe.

Yes.

That's right

We're gonna do a little In and then we're gonna do a little Out

And and count to one two three and in and out

and it feels so nice

and it feels so relaxing

and it doesn't at all feel like you want to put an axe through skull of your best friend slash narcissistic piece of sex addict trash that will get the both of us killed while putting back the feminist agenda ten thousand years because she can't keep her shit in her pants

it's all good

it's not good

it's all

god

oh god

oh god

oh dear god

oh oh ho ho dear god o god o god

>*(While **JESS** continues to disbelieve her anxiety attack into a full-fledged heart attack, **ANGEL** quickly gets into position.)*

>*(And then –)*

The Angel Visits

*(A magnificent **ANGEL** bursts through the ceiling in a magnificentish manner.)*

ANGEL. Greetings, Prophet.

O'NOPE. Okay.

ANGEL. The Great Work begins: The Messenger has arrived.

O'NOPE. Are we sure you are in the right play?

ANGEL. Prophet! I, I, I am the angel from *Angels in America*,

As brought to you by The Ellen McLaughlin on that fateful day of May 1991

The Emma Thompson that justified your Stolen HBO Go ID and password

I have come to you with Messages and Implements of the heavenly kind!

O'NOPE. You are the Angel?

ANGEL. Yes I, I, I am the Angel from Kushner's *Angels in America* and I am very happy to come to you in the stunning likeness of the Beyoncé Knowles Carter you are very welcome it was a challenge to cast her as me but all things are achievable in –

*(Off **O'NOPE***'s *look.)* What.

O'NOPE. Nothing, it's just. You look a lot more like a... Shaunette Renée Wilson[1]?

ANGEL. Really?

O'NOPE. Yeah.

ANGEL. What do you think of this Shaunette Renée Wilson[2]? Is she hot?

---

1. Name of performer playing **ANGEL**
2. Name of performer playing **ANGEL**

O'NOPE. *(Encouraging.)* I think she's alright.

ANGEL. Alright? Just…alright?

> *(**ANGEL** does a special Angel wish-giving swish, with special Angel sound effects.)*

How about now.

O'NOPE. Yeah…no…sorry. Still Shaunette Renée Wilson[3]

ANGEL. Crap. Well no matter. The likeness is mere packaging. It's the insides that matter.

Come inside, into my heavenly angelic bod bod bod!

O'NOPE. Right now?

ANGEL. I, I, I am the Angel with eight vaginas and many much more dicks.

O'NOPE. What, ow, no, I don't get off on penetration.

ANGEL. I, I, I am so much more than just penetration.

> *(**ANGEL** turns their many much more dicks on vibrate and resumes.)*

Prophet. Come! And then Come some more! And then some more after that! And / then some more and more and more!

WILLY. Nooooooooooooooooooooooooooo!!!!!!!!!!!!!!

---

3. Name of performer playing **ANGEL**

Challenge Accepted

(Back at Willy and Sapph's place.)

WILLY. I should have said no! No no no no no – You may not sexually harass my wife who is dressed as my brother-in-law who does not exist! No!

SAPPH. Yeah no. That was wild.

WILLY. Yes. I know. I am so sorry. I did warn you! Why didn't you listen to me, baby? You just had to ignore me and strut out the door looking as cute as one of the Hemsworth brothers in a penguin onesie, you were basically Asking for it OhMyGod NO. No, it is not your fault. I am not victim-blaming you. I'm better than that.

SAPPH. Do you think she knew?

WILLY. Knew what?

SAPPH. That I was your wife.

WILLY. Was? You are my wife.

SAPPH. She totally knew. She could smell the need miles away, I'll bet.

WILLY. Need?

SAPPH. But she played along. And played me up. Then had her way with me.

WILLY. But you didn't, I mean, did you Like it?

SAPPH. Of course. Not. What a woman, Willy. Those piercing eyes, massive biceps. What a thrilling, ly terrible woman.

WILLY. I know. I am so sorry baby.

SAPPH. She knew everything. Where to touch at what speed with what pressure, and at the very end of that unending kiss, to be so bold as to bite my tongue!? To almost draw blood. If she were not your Commanding Officer, Willy I would've slapped her in the face. And she Knew I wanted to. But she Knew I couldn't. And she Knew that this kind of power play is exactly what rushes my senses How? UGH. It's. So. Good.

WILLY. It sounds like you liked it.

SAPPH. No! So good in a hateful way. Like, she is very good, at being horrible. I feel very violated. I am so deeply upset, actually, that I feel like I need to see her again.

WILLY. I don't think that's a good idea.

SAPPH. Why not?

WILLY. Just, she thinks you have leprosy.

SAPPH. I had a sense, that maybe she knew I wasn't sick with a disease last seen in Ancient Rome?

WILLY. You think she knew all along?

She knew all along!

SAPPH. That's why I feel like I want to confront her about –

WILLY. You know what you're right.

SAPPH. I know! I am!

WILLY. We should complain.

SAPPH. We should! We? Should?

WILLY. Yes. We should file a formal letter of complaint.

SAPPH. A formal letter.

WILLY. Well, not formal, because then it would inevitably go up to my dad and I know he won't take kindly to my lack of control over my own wife's need to dress in drag. I'd hate to have him think that I enjoy women in men's clothing!

SAPPH. There's a lot going on inside there, huh?

WILLY. Yes. We should write an informal, but formally worded, letter of complaint.

(**WILLY** *gets paper and pen.*)

Okay, Mrs. Memnon. Hit me with the good stuff.

(**SAPPH** *wants to hit him with other things, not good stuff.*)

SAPPH. "Dear Shane,"

WILLY. Shane?

SAPPH. What.

WILLY. It's just, familiar? I don't even call her by her first name.

SAPPH. Dear Lieutenant?

WILLY. Better, but how about we lose the Dear.

SAPPH. Okay.

WILLY. Got it. Should I read you what we've got so far?

SAPPH. Sure.

WILLY. *(Very sternly.)* Lieutenant.

SAPPH. Great.

WILLY. This is fun. What next?

SAPPH. "Lieutenant. This afternoon when I suffered your rather surprising kiss –"

WILLY. How about nix "surprising," replace with "terrible, and reprehensibly inappropriate"

SAPPH. K.

WILLY. "...prehensibly...inappropriate kisses"

SAPPH. It was just the one kiss.

WILLY. Oh it looked like a lot more.

SAPPH. You were counting?

WILLY. And then how about "I will have you know that I am terribly upset, as is my dear William, to learn of your twisted and gross obsession with me and my pre-leprosy face."

SAPPH. I don't know that we need to keep the leprosy thing going.

WILLY. Oh yeah. You're right. "obsession with me and my pre-married face."

SAPPH. Why, you think she wouldn't be obsessed with my post-married face?

WILLY. Do you want her to be?

SAPPH. "I am lucky to have a very wonderful husband unaffected with jealousy,"

WILLY. "Else I wonder if you'd still even be walking with two unbroken limbs."

SAPPH. Are you threatening to break the limbs of your commanding officer?

WILLY. No you are threatening that I might, if I weren't such a non-jealous husband.

"I ask you to please keep your horny disgusting lesbian-turned-straight-person lust away from me. Know that I hate and detest you as much as I love my husband and my honor.

Sincerely, Mrs. William Memnon. Jr."

SAPPH. Wow. You just, whipped that out.

WILLY. I know, I surprise myself sometimes. I should write more.

SAPPH. It has the feeling of, like an eighteenth-century housewife being forced by her jealous violent husband to write a mean letter to her beautiful lover, against her will –

WILLY. Huh. Really?

SAPPH. Really.

WILLY. Yeah I guess you're right. It really has narrative potential. Do you think I should turn it into something more? Like, a novel or something?

SAPPH. Yes. That is exactly what I meant.

WIFE. *(On paper cup.)* Hello? Willy are you there?

WILLY. Oh it's my mother.

WIFE. *(On paper cup.)* William Iphigenio Memnon, pick up the cup, I need to ask you something.

WILLY. *(On paper cup.)* Mom, you have to say over.

WIFE. *(On paper cup.)* Who is Saphastian?

WILLY. *(On paper cup.)* Mom, you're not doing it right you have to ring the bell, and you have to say over.

WIFE. *(On paper cup.)* Is it your friend? Why did Horne kiss him?

WILLY. *(On paper cup.)* What? How do you know that?

WIFE. *(On paper cup.)* No matter. It's not me, but the ladies want to know who is Saphastian and why was he kissing –

WILLY. *(On paper cup.)* It wasn't her! Him! He didn't kiss her, she kissed him! Right Sapph?

SAPPH. I...

WIFE. *(On paper cup.)* She kissed him. So it is true! But who is this Saphastian –

GENERAL. *(On paper cup.)* Woman! I warned you about misusing government equipment to make personal calls –

WIFE. *(On paper cup.)* This isn't government equipment it's a paper cup!

GENERAL. *(On paper cup.)* It's a Government Paper Cup!

Willy, what was she saying?

WILLY. *(On paper cup.)* Sir! You have to say, um, over, sir, over.

WIFE. *(On paper cup.)* Leave him alone you're just jealous he has a wife who likes him!

GENERAL. *(On paper cup.)* Don't push me, Clytemnestra.

WIFE. *(On paper cup.)* Don't say my name like you know me! You don't know me!

GENERAL. *(On paper cup.)* Cly, put down the Walkie Talkie.

WIFE. *(On paper cup.)* It's not a Walkie Talkie. It's. A. Paper. Fucking.

GENERAL. *(On paper cup.)* Cly, no –

WIFE. *(On paper cup.)* Cup!!

> *(**WILLY**'s paper cup string goes lax and the cute little bell falls to the floor.)*

WILLY. Ugh. She broke it again. The General gets so upset when he doesn't have direct connection to me at all times. But I don't want to leave you when you're so vulnerable, after writing this difficult content.

ANGEL. Inspiration can arrive from a variety of sources. A moment of solitude. A memory of a kiss. The magnificent presence of an Angel bearing the likeness of the very great actor Shaunette Renée Wilson.[1]

> *(A Jingle of inspiration [It would be nice if it was the **ANGEL** making the inspirational Jingle sound.])*

SAPPH. You should go. I'll be okay.

---

1. Name of actor playing **ANGEL**.

WILLY. You sure? It'll just take a minute.

SAPPH. Absolutely.

WILLY. We just need to hook up a new government paper cup.

SAPPH. Urgent work. Please. I understand.

WILLY. Okay. I'll be right back. I'm sorry.

(*A sweet married-people kiss.*)

(*He exits.*)

(**SAPPH** *pulls out a new blank page.*)

(*Another Jingle of inspiration.*)

SAPPH. Dear Shane...

I love re–

(**WILLY** *comes back.*)

(**SAPPH** *eats her paper.*)

WILLY. Sorry, I just wanted to...where's the letter we wrote?

(**SAPPH** *points to it on the desk.*)

Great. I just wondered if maybe my folks would agree with the whole writing a novel thing. Won't hurt to ask right? I mean, maybe not, I don't want them to be like, you can't be an artist you're not good enough and you'll starve to death and we'd rather take trips to Bali over paying for your groceries till you're forty, But also I don't know maybe they'll be supportive?

(**SAPPH** *gives him a thumbs up.*)

You're right. I should give them a chance to see me for who I really am. Thank you Sapph. I love you.

(A sweet married-people kiss.)

(He leaves.)

*(**SAPPH** locks the door, spits out her balled-up letter.)*

SAPPH. Times like this I wonder if marrying for money and status is really worth it.

(She pulls out a new blank page and re-begins her missive.)

*(Delightful sounds happen while **SAPPH** writes...reads, loves.)*

Mm mm, I'm so good.

(Writes...giggles, loves...moans with delight.)

Mm mm, how does she do it?

(Writes...does a little jig that one does when the words you are coming up with just flow out of you and gurgle with joy and authenticity like a newborn babe.)

Uh huh, Uh yeah

My writing makes me wet

Uh huh, Uh yeah

My writing makes me wet

Uh huh, Uh yeah

(At some point during this wet writing dance, the paper cup has been pulled taut.)

My writing makes me wet so wet

My writing will make you so wet

My writing makes me wet so

(Sound of door being tugged.)

(From behind the door –)

WILLY. Sapphy? Why is the door locked?

SAPPH. Hold on!

(**SAPPH** *folds her letter, sealing it.*)

(She unlocks the door.)

WILLY. Why did you lock the door?

SAPPH. I um, I was scared.

WILLY. Oh it's okay, I'm here now.

SAPPH. Did they like the letter?

WILLY. I um, didn't have a chance to bring it up.

SAPPH. I'm sorry.

(**SAPPH** *takes his letter.*)

WILLY. Thank you.

*(Hidden from his view, **SAPPH** switches out the letters, to give **WILLY** her own.)*

SAPPH. Okay. Here.

You go tell that nasty woman exactly what I mean to say to her.

WILLY. Aye, aye Wife!

(He leaves.)

Soap Collection

> (**HORNE** *gives herself and her* Shakespeare *a pre-merry peptalk.*)

HORNE. Alright Willy. It's just you and me again. Again I come to you with baby tickles.

Unleash your power upon me, as you have done for Merry Wives throughout centuries Willy. It's time. Release my tickles.

> (**HORNE** *is excited to begin her climb up this lust mountain.*)

> (*When from the darkness a figure emerges –*)

WIFE. Tell me it's not true.

HORNE. AAH!

WIFE. Who is mister Saphastian.

HORNE. What are you doing here Clytemnestra.

WIFE. You know why I am here.

HORNE. I cannot give you what you came for.

For it is true, what they say of me. I am a ruined woman.

WIFE. I don't believe it. And I need you to not believe it. Gay conversion therapy is not real. Find your inner truth, believe in your true urges, love yourself as who you are and feel it in yourself to love me like a true lover of vagina Please Shane!

HORNE. I'm sorry Cly. I have been reformed.

WIFE. Let me re-reform you.

HORNE. No not yet, I need time for the conflict to flower

WIFE. I don't care what you need I need sex.

HORNE. Cly! You can't just come into a person's tent and demand sex.

WIFE. Give me sex!

HORNE. I can't! I am straight!

(Thunder and lightning!)

(Maybe **O'NOPE**'s *head appears somewhere and watches the thunder pass. And then leaves.)*

Please. Let me internalize my self-hatred so it can manifest in secret taboo sexual behavior that will result in a shameful merry of my own. Let me be straight!

WIFE. I see.

HORNE. You do see?

WIFE. That's how we want to play it today. We are just a coupla straight-ass ladies, having some straight-ass explorations of the female condition, in a hostile environment –

HORNE. Oh.

WIFE. Ah, you like that, huh, do you?

HORNE. How hostile?

WIFE. Very.

HORNE. But like, describe it. Like, if your husband finds out, what exact plot point will occur? Will he knife me in my sleep? Will he send battalions to blow my tent to dust –

WIFE. What? No. He doesn't know I'm here. To be honest I think he's relieved someone's doing his job –

HORNE. I need stakes! I need bigger – I need you to put it in a way that helps me see –

WIFE. Shut up and put yours this-a-way.

HORNE. You don't care about my Merries do you, Mrs. Memnon.

WIFE. Say that again.

HORNE. No! I won't! I want my orgasm.

WIFE. SAY IT.

HORNE. Mrs. Memnon.

(**WIFE** *melts.*)

WIFE. Hmmmlmmmlerh.

HORNE. You are in need.

WIFE. Yes.

HORNE. Mrs. Memnon,

(**WIFE** *melts.*)

WIFE. Hmmmlmmmlerh!

HORNE. That is why you have come –

WIFE. I have come.

HORNE. and yes, we will have you come again.

WIFE. Come again

HORNE. Mrs. –

GENERAL. Mrs. Memnon? Is that you?

WIFE. Nooooooo!

GENERAL. Mrs. Memnon! What are you doing here? I thought you went to Willy's to help with the laundry.

WIFE. Noooooo.

HORNE. It's my fault General. I have distracted your dear wife. I asked her to come –

WIFE. to come

GENERAL. To come?

HORNE. In. To come in, to my place of residence, and she –

WIFE. almost came

HORNE. – in!

WIFE. So close

HORNE. She came in so close to here, where I have, my collection.

GENERAL. What collection?

WIFE. So… / close…

HORNE. Soaps. It is a straight woman hobby, General, to collect soaps. And I was about to show her my straight woman collection of soaps, isn't that right Mrs. Memnon? You want to see my soaps.

WIFE. Soaps. I wish to see – …soaps! Yes. A whole collection of just soaps. We straight women do this. Where is your collection?

HORNE. The bathroom closet, of course. Shall we go in then?!

(**HORNE** *pushes her through to a bathroom.*)

(*To* **WIFE.**) Lock it.

(*She does, leaving* **HORNE** *and* **GENERAL** *locked out of the bathroom.*)

Oh!

GENERAL. What!

HORNE. I can't open it! Mrs. Memnon –

(**WIFE** *melts.*)

WIFE. Hmmmlmmmlerh…

GENERAL. Wife! Are you alright in there?

HORNE. It seems the door is jammed, Mrs. Memnon!

(**WIFE** *melts.*)

WIFE. Hmmmlmmmlerh!

GENERAL. She is in pain! We must do something!

HORNE. Mrs. Memnon!

(**WIFE** *melts.*)

WIFE. Hmmmlmmmlerhlerhlerh!

HORNE. I'm coming around the back!

GENERAL. Hold it tight Wife! She'll get into you the back way!

(**HORNE** *disappears.*)

(*Enter* **FEMALE SOLDIER** *[played by* **ANGEL***].*)

FEMALE SOLDIER (ANGEL). Lieutenant? I heard the news, this is not acceptable –

GENERAL. Captain Wantsome!

FEMALE SOLDIER (ANGEL). General! I didn't expect to see you here, sir!

GENERAL. It is my wife. It seems she is stuck behind Lieutenant Horne's bathroom door.

FEMALE SOLDIER (ANGEL). Where is the Lieutenant?

GENERAL. She's gone into her the back way.

FEMALE SOLDIER (ANGEL). The back way, sir?

(*Enter* **ANOTHER FEMALE SOLDIER** *[played by* **SAPPH***].*)

ANOTHER FEMALE SOLDIER (SAPPH). Shane? Shane what's this nonsense that you have convert–

GENERAL. Lieutenant Wantmore!

ANOTHER FEMALE SOLDIER (SAPPH). General! Captain! Is everything alright?

GENERAL. The door jammed while they were perusing a soap collection. This whole camp is just falling apart.

FEMALE SOLDIER (ANGEL). Or is it your marriage.

GENERAL. What was that?

> *(Enter* **YET ANOTHER FEMALE SOLDIER** *[played by* **O'NOPE***].)*

YET ANOTHER FEMALE SOLDIER (O'NOPE). Horne! Say it isn't so!

GENERAL. Sergeant WantItSoBadLikeYouWantATaco BellAtTwoAM! The door is jammed. We're trying to get Mrs. Memnon back.

FEMALE SOLDIER (ANGEL). Try as we may, seems some beavers will go their beaver way.

ANOTHER FEMALE SOLDIER (SAPPH). Oh! So, it's not – coz I heard...

YET ANOTHER FEMALE SOLDIER (O'NOPE). Me too I heard!

GENERAL. No no, my wife was browsing Horne's Soap Collection.

> *(Door opens, and* **WIFE** *emerges, sea-legged and holding a bar of Irish Spring.[1])*

WIFE. My darling. Lieutenant has so generously gifted me this soap from her collection.

HORNE. I'm just happy it is to your liking, Mrs. Memnon.

WIFE. It was hard to get but I'm glad we took the time to choose the right one.

---

1. A license to produce *Merry Me* does not include a license to publicly display any branded logos or trademarked images. Licensees must acquire rights for any logos and/or images or create their own.

HORNE. Oh it wasn't too hard, was it, Mrs. Memnon?

WIFE. No I guess it's been rather, delightfully moist.

ANOTHER FEMALE SOLDIER (SAPPH). I'd love some moist soap myself, actually, if you are giving them out freely, Lieutenant?

FEMALE SOLDIER (ANGEL). Same.

YET ANOTHER FEMALE SOLDIER (O'NOPE). I love soap I love soap so much.

HORNE. You know, I would love to but I think I'm pretty fresh out of soaps for the moment.

FEMALE SOLDIER (ANGEL). How about we go have a look anyway, hey Shane?

YET ANOTHER FEMALE SOLDIER (O'NOPE). Just a wee look? A wee lather?

GENERAL. What is it with women and their obsession with toiletries?

(**HORNE** *gives him a helpless shrug.*)

Well I'm off to do more important manly General things, get thee to home, Wife!

(*He is gone.*)

SOLDIERS. Well?

(**HORNE** *gives up.*)

HORNE. Come on, let's go.

(*They are led into the bathroom.*)

(*Meanwhile* **ANGEL** *takes off her* **LADY SOLDIER** *wig and returns to us as the* **ANGEL.**)

ANGEL. You like my wig?

Love a good wig.

ANGEL. Such magical things, wigs are, no?

>One minute I'm like Prophet! Come into my bod bod bod

>And then pop on a wig suddenly I'm like

>hey hey I'm Captain Wantsome, you want some?

>It's a bit itchy

>But a good itch, right?

>It Should itch, to pretend to be someone you are not.

>I can tell you, as an Angel who has appeared in a few plays already.

>It requires a great deal of discomfort to perform to be someone you are not for the benefit for someone else.

>But ever since that day young Kushner imagined us into this delightful narrative device we the Angels all agreed that this was a very addictive, if not the most effective way to convey our messages and implements. And this time our message is really pretty good –

O'NOPE. Angel?

ANGEL. Oh, my Prophet calls. Ready for the best scene of the play?

Angel Post-Coital

O'NOPE. Angel?

ANGEL. Yes dear Prophet.

O'NOPE. Did you just Virgin Mary me? Will I beget a son?

ANGEL. No Prophet. We are still getting feedback on that tactic. And it's not all been super positive.

O'NOPE. Will I beget a daughter then?

ANGEL. No Prophet there will be no more begetting.

O'NOPE. Angel then what will happen to me now that I have been taken advantage of several times in all bodily orifices via all geographical directions by a heavenly being?

ANGEL. It is not about what will happen to you, but what you must make happen.

O'NOPE. Oh, like a quest? Like a heavenly quest?

ANGEL. Yes, Prophet.

O'NOPE. Is it like a part-time heavenly quest? Because honestly, I have a pretty full calendar especially since the Blackout, you know, no one can call their moms and watch porn and inevitably they have only themselves to watch and you know what That can do to a person, especially if your job is to kill –

ANGEL. Do not be afraid of such earthly worries, Prophet. The successful completion of the quest will lift the Blackout from the Island and your calendar will free up considerably.

O'NOPE. Oh woah. My quest is going to lift the Blackout? That's a pretty substantial, quest, for a pretty first-time quest-haver, no?

ANGEL. Well, you are a pretty substantial Prophet, Prophet.

O'NOPE. Aw, Ange…

(*A sweet moment of inter-species intimacy.*)

So tell me more. How am I so substantial?

ANGEL. Prophet, we the Angels from *Angels in America* have been watching

We've watched the Ocean as he was forced to transport war, colonialism and European STDs

We've watched the Land as her trees were razed, waters fracked

We've watched an infinity of disasters,

We've watched an infinity of stupid choices

We watched *Avengers: Infinity War* and also more recently *Avengers: Endgame* and they were both wonderfully engaging movies.

O'NOPE. I don't really care for Marvel actually.

ANGEL. Anyway so that is how we came to this our New Message: Die.

O'NOPE. Die? Why?

ANGEL. What do you mean why? Surely you know, things are not going very well for humans.

The capacity to overcome despair, is not growing as fast as your capacity to create it, and the Merries have been dwindling.

After a panicked meeting we initiated the Great Blackout to buy time to find the solution and the solution is Prophet, it's just getting really crowded here is all. According to Angel Virginia, all humans need a room of one's own. You see? You need more room for the Merries to grow.

O'NOPE. So to make room for Merries we should all die?

ANGEL. Not all, just half. Like I said, we were greatly inspired by *Avengers: Infinity War*, and we agree that fifty percent reduction is a good place to start. And You, our chosen Prophet, will take the population of humans to fifty percent, just like the ugly CGI giant did with his glitter glove.

O'NOPE. A glitter glove?

ANGEL. The giant had a glittering glove? With Infinity Stones? And then he did a little,

> (**ANGEL** *gives a flourish giant glove gesture.*)

and then half of humanity painlessly drifted off into dust.

O'NOPE. Yeah sorry I definitely skipped this movie.

ANGEL. That's fine. We the Angels did some research and turns out: Infinity Stones are not a real thing, death is not painless, and bloodshed requires muscle. So. Hope you have been working out.

> (*Heavenly sounds happen and an axe hovers in the air.*)

O'NOPE. The heavenly angels have chosen a female psychiatrist to kill off half of humanity with an axe.

ANGEL. Actually humanity in general is doing a damn good job wiping them own selves out with weapons of mass destruction, climate change, general bad diet, but in the interest of death diversity, the Angels have decided we need a more targeted effort to kill off Cisgender Male Species of European descent, as they have spent centuries in building the structure that would nurture and protect their kind. So that's where we shall begin.

> (*The hovering axe squirts out a little flag from the handle.*)

ANGEL. This is your first assignment.

> (**O'NOPE** *cautiously approaches the axe and being sure to not touch anything, reads the name on the flag.*)

O'NOPE. What? Noooooooooooo! I cannot!!!

ANGEL. It's okay. He sort of knows it is coming. I did him a little visit a few months back.

O'NOPE. But Angel! Private Willy Memnon is my eternal secret sunshine sweet love of mine!

ANGEL. Willy Memnon?

O'NOPE. Yes.

ANGEL. Wow, you really do love a project.

O'NOPE. People get off on different things.

ANGEL. SUBMIT, SUBMIT TO THE WILL OF HEAVEN!

O'NOPE. I do like to submit. But why me Angel?

ANGEL. For too long you have said no to all that life has offered, Dear Prophet. And from today onward you shall be redubbed Jess O'Jes! Say Jes to life! Say Jes to what you are! Be the Prophet! Ignite your queer female rage, let it combust the injustices around you!

O'NOPE. I don't have rage, queer female or otherwise.

ANGEL. Yeah you do. That's how we found you.

O'NOPE. No no, Sorry Ange. I mean, thank you for all the heavenly sex but I'm afraid you got the wrong gal. No rage here.

ANGEL. Okay you gonna make me do this what do you make to a white man's dollar?

O'NOPE. ...Seventy-three cents.[1]

---

1. Please update this statistic according to the gender and ethnicity of your production's **O'NOPE**.

ANGEL. How many years after Democracy was invented did women get to vote?

O'NOPE. Twenty-six centuries.

ANGEL. In the sixty-nine years since its existence how many female directors have been hired to direct a *Shakespeare in the Park*? [2]

O'NOPE. Give me that axe.

(The heavenly axe flies at great speed towards **O'NOPE.***)*

AAARRRRRRRR

(The axe expertly lands itself in **O'NOPE**'s *right hand, like Thor's Hammer.)*

– AAARRRRhuh. Oh.

ANGEL. So?

O'NOPE. So this is how it feels.

ANGEL. How does it feel?

O'NOPE. Powerful.

*(***O'NOPE** *tries out a power axe move.)*

BRRAAAAAAAAAAGH GAKGAKGAK!!! GAKGAKGAK GAK!!!!

It's kinda heavy though.

ANGEL. Go Prophet! Where there is a will, the biceps shall follow.

(Angel voice.) When you overcome the test, you shall know for then, and only then, will the Blackout lift from your Island city, and the General shall have his war, and kill some more!

---

2. Insert local theater joke about gender equity or rather, the lack thereof. If your town has achieved gender parity congratulations and my sincerest apologies that this line might not really land for y'all.

A Pair of Despairs

(The lodgings of Lieutenant Shane Horne.)

*(**HORNE** is a portrait of exhaustion and despair – draped on some furniture, icing her wrist and neck.)*

*(**O'NOPE** is at her doorway, axe in hand.)*

O'NOPE. BRRAAAAAAAAAGH GAKGAKGAK!!!

GAKGAKGAK GAK!!!!

*(**HORNE** doesn't have the energy to look up.)*

HORNE. Hi Jess.

O'NOPE. Hi Shane. How's it going?

HORNE. I am in despair.

O'NOPE. I have an axe.

HORNE. Nice.

O'NOPE. I was actually coming / here to –

HORNE. No. I cannot make you come, not right now Jess.

O'NOPE. I don't need to come I have an axe.

HORNE. And I have despairs. Jess, I have reverted back to my old ways. But now I know. Even an expert mountain climber needs a fellow climber to hoist her up in time of despair. All my life I have been pulling people up their little anthills of pleasure. And not a one of them have the interest nor ability to pull me up anywhere. They don't care about my Merries. I was born to be the Holy Grail but will serve the function of a paper cup to all uncaring unempathizing untalented passersby until I die. If that is so, I might as well die right now. Give me that axe! Why do you have an axe?

O'NOPE. I was trying to tell you, an Angel –

HORNE. No matter, I don't have care for questions and answers of the mortal world. Give me that axe!

O'NOPE. Really?

HORNE. What?

O'NOPE. Why do we always have to talk about you. Why can't we ever talk about me instead? I have despairs, I have anxieties, I have crises of identity. Why is it that it is so hard for you to see me as a person who is as whole and complicated and nuanced as you are? Why?

HORNE. Because you are my therapist. You are different.

O'NOPE. What do you mean?

HORNE. You have, a shimmer about you. A glimmer of a shimmer, giving us a look of defiance, a "I shall stand up for myself goddamit" voice. You have had the sex.

>   (**ANGEL** *gives "it's true she has had the sex" sounds.)*

O'NOPE. Mm hmm.

HORNE. You have had multiples of sex!

>   (**ANGEL** *gives a few more smug "it's true she has had the sex" sounds.)*

O'NOPE. Mm hmm.

HORNE. And you liked it.

ANGEL. She did o lord yes she did.

O'NOPE. Shane. I have been visited by an Angel who gave me forty-seven climaxes consecutively.

>   (**ANGEL** *gives unnecessary amounts of "it's true she has had the sex" sounds.)*

HORNE. What?

O'NOPE. She is the Angel from Kushner's *Angels in America*. She came to tell me that they caused the Blackout, and that I have been chosen as their new Prophet, and so now I have to kill some people.

ANGEL. Not all of you, just half.

HORNE. That is bananas.

O'NOPE. I don't know what to do.

HORNE. Was it mostly tongue or fingers?

O'NOPE. What?

HORNE. Forty-seven? Obviously both. What other toys? Were there toys?

ANGEL & HORNE. There were toys.

HORNE. Do you remember the order of foreplay, did it go top down? bottom up? bottom forward? Although

ANGEL & HORNE. Forty-seven times,

HORNE. It can't be simple I imagine,

ANGEL & HORNE. O Nope.

HORNE. This Angel must have had an intricate path moving through the body,

ANGEL & HORNE. O Jes.

HORNE. I would love to share algorithms, do you have her email?

O'NOPE. I don't think the Angel would give me her email.

HORNE. Don't assume that. You never know till you ask.

ANGEL. Angel_thebestoneatthesexthatiswhyiamhead angel@hotmail.com

O'NOPE. She was an Angel, she was good at the sex, she also told me to murder people Shane.

ANGEL. Not all, just half.

O'NOPE. I can't do that?

HORNE. Of course you can. Women always feel they are underqualified, but in my experience, we can do anything men can do, short of anything requiring upper body strength.

*(**O'NOPE** shows her the axe.)*

O'NOPE. This is what I have to kill with.

HORNE. Oh. That's rough.

O'NOPE. A bit.

HORNE. What do you have to kill?

O'NOPE. Willy Memnon.

HORNE. Well that shouldn't be too hard then.

O'NOPE. Shane!

HORNE. What? He's a weeny. I could help! Ooh let me help let me help!! I could call him to a secluded remote area where we can lock the doors? I could call him here? I could be the lookout while you chop him up?

O'NOPE. Chop him up? Wouldn't it be a single chop, a relatively painless –

*(**WILLY** enters.)*

WILLY. Lieutenant Horne?

HORNE. Oh wow. I'm good. Hello Private!

WILLY. Is it a good time?

HORNE. The most excellent time.

*(Suggestive look to **O'NOPE**.)*

O'NOPE. No! It's not a good time.

WILLY. That's alright Doctor. I won't take up much time. I am here to deliver a letter to Lieutenant Horne and then I will be gone.

HORNE. *(To* **O'NOPE.***)* See? He wants to be gone.

O'NOPE. That's not what he meant!

HORNE. *(To* **WILLY.***)* Is that not what you meant?

WILLY. It's absolutely what I meant. Here it is. The letter from my wife.

She took great offense to your behavior this afternoon, and bids you peruse this letter.

HORNE. Your wife? I thought she wasn't with us?

WILLY. She was, and forgive my forwardness, Ma'am, but I think you knew she was when you went ahead and kissed her anyway in front of her newlywedded husband.

HORNE. Private Drop and give me twenty!

WILLY. Sir yes sir!

(**WILLY** *does. He is not very good at it.*)

(**HORNE** *is like, "Now, Jess, do it now.")*

HORNE. That sweet man was your wife? Why in hell was she dressed like a man? Did you make her?

WILLY. No Ma'am I did not!

(**O'NOPE** *attempts a head chop and fails because she is too far away.*)

HORNE. Private do you have inclination towards sexual immoralities?

WILLY. No Ma'am I do not!

(**O'NOPE** *attempts a head chop and fails because she is too close.*)

HORNE. Why would you dress your wife as a man, and watch as she kisses a woman who is newly straight?

WILLY. She did not kiss you, you kissed her!

(**O'NOPE** *attempts a head chop and fails because she lowers the axe ever so slowly and gently.*)

ANGEL. Oh my god just let gravity do it!

(**WILLY** *is not done with his twenty but is too bedraggled to continue.*)

HORNE. You okay?

WILLY. I'll be fine.

HORNE. You should really work on your upper body strength.

WILLY. Just please read the letter so that I may exit the scene?

(**HORNE** *opens the letter.*)

HORNE. Woah.

WILLY. She means every word, Lieutenant.

HORNE. And you're okay with that?

WILLY. ...Yeah? Why?

Something feels off. May I see that?

HORNE. You may not.

WILLY. Why not?

HORNE. Because. This is my sadness. Please return to your wife, so that I may weep in private, Private.

WILLY. I married a good woman, Ma'am, please let her be who she needs to be.

(*He leaves.*)

O'NOPE. That was actually a pretty good effort don't you think? We'll get him next time. Up top!

(**HORNE** *is not listening.*)

O'NOPE. Shane. You okay?

HORNE. No. I'm afraid not.

(**HORNE** *hands the letter to* **O'NOPE**, *and as she reads.*)

(**SAPPH** *appears, with Special Love Jingle.*)

SAPPH. Dearest Shane,

I love refinement and for me Love has gifted

The splendour and beauty of the sun.

Wealth without it is no safe harbour.

FYI. Sun = You

**Come to me now. Grant me release from this
sorrow.**

Drive away care, I beseech thee O Goddess

Fulfill for me what I yearn to accomplish

Be thou my ally.

devotedly and deliciously yours, Sappho.

O'NOPE. Wow.

HORNE. I know. She's a hottie and does drag and is also a literary genius whose fragments of poetry will outlast millennia of human culture. What do I do. What do I say? I can't match that? Yes I can match that. Think Shane Think.

(**SHANE** *thinks very hard.*)

O'NOPE. You know what I can't be doing this with you right now I have to go kill a man.

HORNE. But before you go what do I say? What do –?

I got it I got it. Yes. How about

Dear Sappho,

> *(Beat drop.)* [1]

I could drink a mug of you.

O'NOPE. A mug?

HORNE. Like it's a metaphor, like, you know, you're a hot steaming mug of hotness and I will drink it all.

O'NOPE. Yeah, but it feels a bit, I don't know, small? What about like, a carafe? A, six pack. A case of wine? I could drink a case of wine of you.

HORNE. Hm. I like mug.

Dear Sappho.

> *(Beat drop.)*

I could drink a mug of you.

I...I will be King

And you...you will be King also.

And so...

Come to my window, sill.

Comingly yours, Horne.

Boom.

> *(Beautiful sounds again.)*

SAPPHO. **In my bosom my heart wildly flutters**

And when on thee I gaze never so little

Bereft am I of all power of utterance

---

1. A license to produce *Merry Me* does not include a performance license for any third-party or copyrighted music. Licensees should create an original composition or use music in the public domain. For further information, please see the Music and Third-Party Materials Use Note on page iii.

SAPPHO. My tongue is useless.

> My ears hear nothing but sounds of winds
> roaring
>
> And all is darkness

O'NOPE. Ho, kay.

> *(Beat drop.)*

HORNE. Hold me closer tiny letter writer

> Lay me down in my military issued bedcot sheets

O'NOPE. Aw Shane, that's actually really sweet.

HORNE. I know. Who even am I anymore?

> Come to my window sill!
>
> *(Beat drop to mega mix,* **ANGEL** *is full-on DJ.[1])*
>
> Or I could come to your window sill!
>
> I'd climb across the mountaintops
>
> Swim all across the ocean blue
>
> Coz I could drink a mug of you
>
> I could drink a tub of you
>
> Olympic regulation size swimming pool of you
>
> Forever and ever
>
> We could be...
>
> We could be...
>
> We could be...?

---

1. A license to produce *Merry Me* does not include a performance license for any third-party or copyrighted music. Licensees should create an original composition or use music in the public domain. For further information, please see the Music and Third-Party Materials Use Note on page iii.

(What could we possibly be? An idea inspired
by the DJ **ANGEL** *says...)*

Pink.

SAPPH. Pink?

HORNE. Yeah Pink

like the inside of your

SAPPH. Maybe

Pink like the tongue that goes down

HORNE. Naughty.

SAPPH. Some like that

HORNE. Uh huh. Do you like that?

SAPPH. Um. Huh. I like that

HORNE. I like that

SAPPH. I like that

HORNE. I like that

ANGEL. I like that

O'NOPE. I love that. I love that so much.

*(**ANGEL** escalates it to a beats/harp remix.)*

SAPPH. Oh it's true

HORNE. I was made for you

SAPPH. Come to my window sill

HORNE. Where is your window sill

SAPPH. Oh I don't know I live in a tent

HORNE. Oh I will find your tent and your window

SAPPH. climb across the mountaintops

Swim all across the ocean blue

HORNE. We're on the same island it won't be that intense

SAPPH. O It's true

HORNE. I was made for you

    And I can drink a

SAPPH. I could drink a thousand frat party upside down keg stands of you

    I will be king

HORNE. And I will be king also

SAPPH. And we shall top the mountains

HORNE. And we shall swim the oceans

TOGETHER. And we shall pink

HORNE. Pink Like the king

SAPPH. Pink Like the everything

TOGETHER. Like the in, the in, the in

    The insi…i…i…de

(And like a miracle, celestial echoes of Merries fill the earth…)

*(****SAPPH**** is here.)*

HORNE. Hello.

SAPPH. Hi.

JESS. I –

HORNE. Bye Jess.

*(****DOCTOR O'NOPE**** leaves while no one acknowledges her departure.)*

SAPPH. Lieutenant Horne.

HORNE. Mister Saphastian.

SAPPH. My dear sister Sappho, god rest her soul, wanted me to return this favor.

From her blistering heart to your iridescent lips.

(Kiss. Much kiss.)

HORNE. Has she then succumbed to the leprosy?

SAPPH. Yeah she's dead.

(Kiss. Much kiss. The kiss develops into something more heated, visceral, physical...)

(Till **SAPPH** *pulls away.)*

That's not it.

HORNE. That's not it?

What's not it.

SAPPH. Sorry, I didn't mean that I just, I thought it would be different

HORNE. Okay...?

SAPPH. I don't know

I don't know what I'm talking about nevermind.

HORNE. No say

SAPPH. Say?

HORNE. Please

SAPPH. I just thought, expected, and maybe what I expected should change

HORNE. No it shouldn't what did you expect

SAPPH. It's like, you are trying to climb a mountain, hoisting me along.

HORNE. I am.

SAPPH. And it feels like, you want me to be your supporting actor in your play of Act One we have sad broken pussy, you cannot do the sex,

HORNE. I do!

SAPPH. to Act Five what had been lost has been recovered by a caring, inquisitive vagina-lover.

HORNE. And you...are not? A caring, inquisitive vagina-lover?

Is this the part of the play where the straight girl has doubts and breaks the heart of the queer heartthrob who after all this time finally opened up their heart?

SAPPH. You opened up your heart?

HORNE. I mean it's closing?

SAPPH. No doubts. I Promise. It's just,

HORNE. It's just?

SAPPH. it's less a climb and more,

campfire, no?

HORNE. Campfire. (??)

SAPPH. You light a match

that finds a ball of shredded paper, catches some kindling,

then maybe something more, longer lasting.

Most of the times it can't, it tries and fails and dies but

sometimes the flame finds a bark, or dried-up branch

the heat moves, eats up the wood, scorching it black

and if the wind blows just the right speed, the right direction that both fuels and protects the flames – suddenly, your whole body is at flamepoint temperature, and it all just

pops.

the tip of your clit, tops of your toes, the veins behind
your eyeballs

pop

I feel

I might die,

but also I want to hold onto it all for as long as I can.

And in that effort, everything

stops

working,

like,

HORNE. pop

SAPPH. yeah.

And then somehow

you remember to breathe again,

and the flames quiet down

but they aren't gone,

HORNE. No,

SAPPH. we're just past peak point

feed it more fuel, give it wind, give it protection and

whoosh

there she goes again

and again

and again

and again

infinitely

as long as you want

SAPPH. as long as you can

as long as you feed it.

HORNE. Oh.

SAPPH. Did you just come a little.

HORNE. Mm hmm. *(Yes.)*

SAPPH. Same.

> *(***SAPPH** *and* **HORNE** *share a moment of quiet, intimate, almost childlike delight.)*

> *(I found you. Hi.)*

Come.

> *(She leads.* **HORNE** *follows.)*

> *(And when they shut the door behind them the impact of their Merries vaccum the air, shake the Earth, break the everything...)*

Willy vs Jess

(And we are in Private Willy's Glamping Tent of Sadness.)

(His place is a mess: strewn with old letters, wedding photographs, empty bottles of alcohol, junk food.)

(He is holed up in the corner among all the chaos, quietly and methodically tearing up letters.)

(There is a mountain of letters.)

*(**O'NOPE** appears in the doorway with her axe.)*

O'NOPE. BRRAAAAAAAAAGH GAKGAKGAK!!!

GAKGAKGAKGAK

*(**O'NOPE** is so alarmed at the state of affairs that she stops her axe power moves.)*

WILLY. Hello Doctor.

O'NOPE. Are you okay?

WILLY. She left.

O'NOPE. Who?

WILLY. My wife.

O'NOPE. How long has she been gone?

WILLY. I don't know. I have lost sense of time. Maybe an hour? Two?

O'NOPE. She might be back, don't you think?

WILLY. I found these letters. From Horne. I've always known, Sapph does not think I am enough for her. I've always known this day will come. And it has.

GENERAL. *(On paper cup.)* Brring Brring. Private Memnon. We have reached a shortage of backup bells and so we are instituting a new call-in technology of mouth sounds. Please confirm with your own Brring Brring. Over.

WIFE. *(On paper cup.)* Brring Brring hi this is your wife from the other room yet again reminding you that this is really fucking dumb. Over.

GENERAL. *(On paper cup.)* Don't you start with me woman, it's your fault all our bells are broken.

WIFE. *(On paper cup.)* That's right blame the wife, for the broken bells and broken balls, but think long and hard about who is to blame for the boy's shrinking pecker.

GENERAL. *(On paper cup.)* We are not discussing my Private's privates on government line!

WIFE. *(On paper cup.)* Jesus Christ I give up.

O'NOPE. You close with your family?

WILLY. My mom. With my dad it's a bit trickier. What's with the axe?

O'NOPE. I have to kill you with it.

WILLY. Huh.

O'NOPE. An Angel came and gave me a lot of sex and then this axe and told me to kill you with it.

WILLY. An Angel?

O'NOPE. I know it sounds crazy but –

WILLY. Did she look like Shaunette Renée Wilson?[1]

O'NOPE. What? Yes?!

WILLY. How many times did you –?

O'NOPE. Forty-seven.

---

1. Name of performer playing **ANGEL**

WILLY. Forty-seven?!

O'NOPE. Yup.

WILLY. Me too forty-seven.

O'NOPE. Hoh.

WILLY. Did it hurt, when she did the –?

O'NOPE. Oh. Oh yeah. Definitely. But like, you know, it was like the good hurt.

(**WILLY** *remembers this fondly.*)

WILLY. Yeah. Yeah it was. It's not easy to be chosen.

O'NOPE. No it's hard.

(They enjoy the comradery of chosen-ness.)

(Then they look at the axe.)

WILLY. So how are we fixing the Blackout?

O'NOPE. Oh.

WILLY. Did she say the Blackout would be fixed if you kill me?

O'NOPE. I'm sorry.

WILLY. That seems extreme. But makes sense.

O'NOPE. Does it?

WILLY. I'm a woke white man. I can come to pretend to understand extremities I do not fully comprehend by mansplaining and then apologizing.

O'NOPE. You got a lot going on inside there, huh.

WILLY. What if I have been conditioned all my life to believe I am excellent above all other types of humans while not really being trained to work as hard? What if I am actually quite medium in talent, tenacity and general interestingness and I know I have not developed a mental capacity to bridge the discrepancy between the genius I self-identify to be and the mediocre lump of ego that I actually am?

O'NOPE. We could start you on some drugs?

GENERAL. *(On paper cup.)* Brring Brring Private Memnon! This is to let you know most other devices have confirmed with their own brring brring. I am still waiting for yours. Over.

WIFE. *(On paper cup.)* Literally no one else has confirmed your dumb game Aga. Leave the boy alone.

GENERAL. *(On paper cup.)* People have confirmed! Captain Wantsome, Lieutenant Wantmore, Sergeant TacoBell,

WIFE. *(On paper cup.)* Horne hasn't confirmed!

GENERAL. *(On paper cup.)* Woman will you drop that obsession with the newly-straight Shane Horne?

WIFE. *(On paper cup.)* It's not an obsession, it is love. I am in love. No one can take that away from me. You can't take that away from me!

GENERAL. *(On paper cup.)* I don't have to! You can't love her! She is straight! Straight! Straight!

WILLY. *(On paper cup.)* Brring Brring she's not straight. She's with Sapph right now probably having incredible sex in her probably pre-set-up Red Room tent. Over.

GENERAL. *(On paper cup.)* Brring Brring what the fuck!? Over!

WIFE. *(On paper cup.)* Brring Brring how do you know this?! Over!

GENERAL. *(On paper cup.)* Brring Brring Willy! Come over right now! Come over and explain to us the scenes I haven't been in since –

*(**WILLY** cuts off the paper cup string on his end.)*

O'NOPE. I really wish you hadn't done that.

WILLY. It's the truth.

O'NOPE. Yes but now your father will be sending his otherwise superb and shapely-shouldered soldier, heretical hetero et cetera et cetera jiu-jitsued into BRAGH GAK GAK GAK ending in a short drug-addled life on the inner city streets. The consequences are very high.

WILLY. I don't care. I am in despair.

O'NOPE. Well, I guess this is helping me with my mission.

WILLY. Did I just unwittingly ignite your rage with my non-woke white person wallowing?

O'NOPE. You did a little.

WILLY. I really wish I knew how to stop doing that.

O'NOPE. We all do.

> (**O'NOPE** *takes up her axe.*)

It's time, William.

WILLY. Okay.

> (**WILLY** *kneels for execution in a very solemn* Game of Thrones *kind of way.*)

> (**O'NOPE** *swings her axe up.*)

AAAAAAAAAAAAAAAAAAAGGGGGGGGGKK KKKK!

O'NOPE. I haven't done it yet.

WILLY. Oh. Sorry. Go ahead.

> (**O'NOPE** *swings her axe up again.*)

AAAAAAAAAAAAAAGGGGGGGGKKKKKK!

O'NOPE. Willy.

WILLY. Oh. Sorry. I don't know why I do that. Okay I'm really ready now.

> (**O'NOPE** *swings her axe up maybe half way.*)

AAAAAAAAAAAAAAAGGGGGGGGGKKKKKKKPLEASE DON'TKILLMESAPPHYHELLLLP!

> (**O'NOPE** *lets her axe down.*)

O'NOPE. Okay this isn't working.

> (**ANGELS** *enter with popcorn.*)

ANGEL. We the Angels came to watch. It seemed you were near the climax point.

O'NOPE. We are not.

WILLY. We are not?

ANOTHER ANGEL (WIFE). It's page seventy-four. What's taking so long?

O'NOPE. Angels I wish to return this to you.

YET ANOTHER ANGEL (GENERAL). Why? What's wrong with it?

O'NOPE. Nothing's wrong with it. I just, I don't want to live the life of a person who has rage-killed another person who is screaming for his life. I still want the job, as Prophet? Couldn't I just, couldn't I destroy him with my love?

ANOTHER ANGEL (WIFE). Love?

ANGEL. We the Angels are dubious.

O'NOPE. I could domesticate him, make him take out the recycling, fix the dishwasher while making him think this is somehow a show of his magnificent masculinity, no?

I could win constitutional parody with the argument that he is the one that is being oppressed by the gender-biased laws, and when Roe v. Wade gets overturned half a century later I can keep trying, keep organizing, keep up the hope that science and biology might be law one day, I won't stop coming up with new ideas for *Shakespeare in the Park* as the four hundred and fifty-sixth female director who pitched and was rejected, I won't stop.[1] Just me not stopping, can that not be my axe?

ANGEL. The Angels are dubious.

ANOTHER ANGEL (WIFE). The Angels prefer the axe.

Or if Doctor O'Nope is uncertain about her upper body strength, we the Angels totally get it –

YET ANOTHER ANGEL (GENERAL). – and could try to find a bow and arrow!

Like the *Hunger Games*!

> *(The* **ANGELS** *mmmm and aaaah because they liked this movie a lot also.)*

WILLY. I should go.

O'NOPE. Okay. We'll do this later. Call me if you need to talk more, okay?

WILLY. No I mean I should go. You won't have to rage-kill if I depression-die.

O'NOPE. Oh. Are you sure that's how it works?

WILLY. Yes. The Angels are not wrong. Men like me have sat on the throne and ruined everything. I need to be gone, I need to make space for this brave new world. I have to give up my space. Completely.

---

1. Insert another local theater joke about gender equity or rather, the lack thereof. If your town has achieved gender parity congratulations and my sincerest apologies that this line might not really land for y'all.

*(In his impassioned fervor, **WILLY** has taken center stage, blocking **O'NOPE**.)*

O'NOPE. Willy, you're, um –

WILLY. Oh. Did I just take up space while yelling about giving up space again?

O'NOPE. You did a little.

WILLY. I really wish I knew how to stop doing that.

O'NOPE. I don't know. Just like, read the room.

WILLY. Read the room. Huh.

ANGEL. How do we feel about this turn of events?

ANOTHER ANGEL (WIFE). I still prefer the axe.

YET ANOTHER ANGEL (GENERAL). Don't give up just yet. This could still go many different ways

ANGELS. Free will. Ugh.

*(The **ANGELS** roll their heavenly eyes.)*

*(**SAPPH** and **HORNE** enter.)*

SAPPH. Willy dear the Lieutenant and I have some news to –

Oh hello! Willy! Your friends? Who is everyone?

WILLY. Hey Sapphy.

SAPPH. Darling why do you look so down?

WILLY. This is Doctor O'Nope who is my shrink and over there are the Angels from *Angels in America* who asked the Doctor to kill me. But I'm just going to jump off a building so she doesn't have to live the life of a rage-murderer.

O'NOPE. You know Angels, I just feel like there is a different solution to the dwindling Merries problem than asking sad people to jump off buildings.

ANGEL. Well, this is the test run so we should run it and do feedback after. Okay?

(**O'NOPE** *is dubious.*)

(*Everyone else looks at* **WILLY**.)

WILLY. Oh. That's me. Okay.

Goodbye. Goodbye World.

Goodbye Naval Basecamp on an Island Not Far from Enemy Nation's Most Vulnerable Coast Cities.

Oh, Earth, you're too wonderful for –

O'NOPE. Willy, you're, um –

WILLY. Yeah, no I felt that. Read the room.

O'NOPE. Good job.

WILLY. Bye Doctor.

(*And with that,* **WILLY** *flings himself off into an unknown abyss.*)

(*Long silence, and then a splash in the distance.*)

(*Silence. And then:*)

O'NOPE. Oh interesting look at that, the extra space isn't really doing anything for my Merries or my rage. Funny how that is revealed to us now that a whole man is dead.

ANGEL. Thank you for the feedback, Prophet. Anyone else want the axe?

(*Nobody responds, but hopefully also no one from the audience responds…[1]*)

---

[1] In the event an audience member wants the axe, here are my offers to not give it away: "Hm, not really Prophet material / Seems to lack upper body strength / [any other ad-libbed response that seems appropriate to your community]"

ANGEL. I feel like this new mission doesn't really have the momentum we had hoped for.

OTHER ANGELS. No.

ANGEL. What are we doing wrong here?

YET ANOTHER ANGEL (GENERAL). I told you we should've gone *Hunger Games.* Long-distance murder requires way less conversation.

ANOTHER ANGEL (WIFE). Yeah it seems the dying takes a lot longer when they like each other.

ANGEL. What about the destroying with love thing? Is that a thing?

YET ANOTHER ANGEL (GENERAL). Unverified.

ANOTHER ANGEL (WIFE). I'll have my interns look into it.

ANGEL. Yes please do and perhaps this time Netflix should not be their main source of research.

ANOTHER ANGEL (WIFE). Understood. Apologies.

ANGEL. No no. Cheer up, Angels! As Angel Samuel always likes to say: try again, fail again, fail better. We must go back to the drawing board and in the next few decades, come back in another new play.

YET ANOTHER ANGEL (GENERAL). In the meantime shall we let them have war, travel, and porn?

ANGEL. Sure why not.

(*People's phones start bleeping.*)

HORNE. Oh we have service again.

ANGEL. Thank you Prophet. The Blackout is lifted. The General shall have his war.

(*The* **ANGELS** *ascend.*)

HORNE. Are you sad?

SAPPH. I think so a little? I am very moved by my ex-husband's self-sacrifice.

HORNE. I will remember your ex-husband's angelic sacrifice always, as I consummate my desires to the one and only love of his life while raising his child as my own –

SAPPH. We did not have a child.

HORNE. Oh good. But if you did I would let it run into my arms at the end of the play.

SAPPH. So kind.

HORNE. Well, if there is no child running into my arms to signal the end of the play I guess there's only one thing left to do.

(**HORNE** *gets down on one knee.*)

SAPPH. Excuse?

HORNE. You look shocked. Should I be offended?

SAPPH. I just didn't take you for the marrying type.

HORNE. I'm not. But how else will people know that this was a comedy?

SAPPH. Is that a good reason for two adults to go into a lifelong commitment?

HORNE. I don't know any good reason for two adults to go into a lifelong commitment.

But I like you.

SAPPH. I like you too.

HORNE. So it's a yes?

SAPPH. Maybe let's go on a date first.

(*Kiss.*)

HORNE. Maybe should it be an open relationship?

(Kiss.)

SAPPH. Maybe can we have a Red Room?

HORNE. Who doesn't have a Red Room?

(Kiss.)

O'NOPE. This is gonna take a while. Can we clear the stage
so I can do the epilogue?

(Soft light narrows to **O'NOPE**.*)*

Epilogue

O'NOPE.   The General had his war, and successfully re-erected his penis, both things distracting him from the small domestic fights he used to pick to try to help his dick feel big. Unfortunately, he also killed many people during the process and was tried for his war crimes soon thereafter. Clytemnestra has divorced him since, and lives in a lesbian commune.

Willy did not die. He landed in Shane's hot tub, broke a few bones and his ego but came back a new man. And after many conversations about room reading, we dated. And after many more conversations about room reading, we broke up. We're still good friends tho, I got him into hot yoga.

I found my Merries after all. Turns out, I had them with me all along.

I stand before you today proud and merry to say I am single, available, hot as a motherfucker, and if you are an emotionally unavailable project of a person please leave your number with the box office.

The Angels never came back, but I kept the axe.

A good reminder

that I was once angry enough to carry it

that Willy was once sad enough to want it

but mostly it's just a good hefty weight to hold the door open when I let the dogs out at night.

It's still hard to be alive some days.

It's humiliating to be so imperfect.

To fear so deeply,

To hate so sharply,

O'NOPE. To believe you'll never be merry enough, ever.

But to those of you who are nodding, I say.

Go to Lowe's and get yourself an axe.

It can just bear the weight enough

to hold the door open

on those breezy summer nights.

Good night.

Be merry.

End of Play